THE RED WEDDING

SWARUP NILESH KADAM

Contents

Preface

"Yato Dharmas Tato Jayaḥ"

(Where there is Dharma there is victory)

They say history is written by the victors. But what of those who died with their names buried in silence, their blood soaking the stones of forgotten halls? This book is their answer.

The Red Wedding began not as a tale of vengeance, but as a meditation on trust, ambition, and the price of loyalty in a world ruled by swords and shadows. Inspired by the murkier sides of power and war, this story follows characters who are not wholly innocent, yet undeserving of the brutal fate that greets them. It explores what happens when honor is met with treachery, and how one betrayal can ignite a cycle of destruction.

Writing this book was an act of catharsis—an attempt to wrestle with the duality of justice and vengeance, the thin line between duty and destruction. It was forged in late nights and long silences, where the characters demanded to be heard.
If you're reading this, thank you for stepping into their world. It's not a gentle place—but perhaps, in its honesty, it is a necessary one.
—**Swarup**

Acknowledgements

To those who kept me grounded while I wandered the halls of vengeance and war:

First and foremost, to my family—thank you for your unwavering belief in my storytelling, even when my tales turned dark and stormy. Your patience and encouragement gave me the space to finish this story the way it deserved.

To my closest friends and early readers—you read rough drafts filled with chaos and still saw the bones of a story worth telling. Your feedback was fierce and honest, exactly what I needed.

To the creators and worlds that inspired me—George R. R. Martin, Glen Cook, and the lore-drenched songs of history—you taught me that tragedy can carry truth.

And finally, to the reader holding this book: thank you for choosing to journey into the Red Wedding's Hall. May its ghosts haunt you long after the last page.

Before We Begin...

I would like to give the reader a quick note on chronology. A majority of the chapters in this book take place parallel to each other, meaning they essentially take place within the same time frame. This is mostly prevalent in part 1 although there are instances in part 2 as well. The reader should keep in mind that the chapters are separated by viewpoint, rather than chronology.

Prologue

In the heart of Manchester, where the River Irwell meandered lazily through the bustling city streets, lies a tale woven from the threads of love, ambition, and betrayal. It is a tale as old as time itself, yet one that continues to unfold with each passing moment, leaving in its wake a trail of broken hearts and shattered dreams.

At the center of this tale stands Sylas Wilson, a man of wealth and influence, whose meteoric rise from humble beginnings had earned him the admiration and envy of all who knew him. With his piercing gaze and charming smile, Sylas was a man who commanded attention, whose every word carried the weight of authority and power.

But beneath the facade of success and prosperity, Sylas harbored a secret—a secret that threatened to unravel the carefully constructed tapestry of his life. For months, he had been carrying on an affair with Scarlet La Quelle, his beautiful and enigmatic subordinate, their forbidden love hidden from the prying eyes of the world.

Yet, despite the danger posed by their illicit romance, Sylas could not bring himself to end it. Scarlet was a temptation too great to resist, a flame that burned with a fierce intensity, consuming him with every stolen moment they shared together.

And so, as Sylas prepared to marry another woman, his heart torn between duty and desire, he found himself ensnared in a web of deceit and deception from which there could be no escape.

But Sylas was not the only one harboring secrets on this fateful day. For Autumn Evans, the bride-to-be, carried within her heart a burden of her own—a burden born of duty and obligation, rather than love.

Autumn had always been a dutiful daughter, obedient to the wishes of her mother and sisters, her own desires relegated to the shadows. And so, when the opportunity arose for her to marry Sylas Wilson, a man of wealth and influence, she had seized it with both hands, desperate to escape the confines of her sheltered existence.But as the wedding day drew near, doubts crept into Autumn's mind, doubts born of uncertainty and fear. For she knew that her union with Sylas was based not on love, but on convenience—a business transaction masquerading as a fairy tale romance.

Yet, despite her misgivings, Autumn could not bring herself to abandon her duty. The weight of expectation bore down on her like a leaden cloak, suffocating her with each passing moment.

And so, as she prepared to walk down the aisle to meet her fate, Autumn forced a smile onto her lips, hiding the turmoil that raged within her soul. For today was a day of celebration, a day to put aside her doubts and fears and embrace the promise of a brighter tomorrow.

But amidst the joy and excitement that filled the air, shadows lurked in the corners, their presence a harbinger of the darkness that lay ahead. For in the heart of Manchester, where love and ambition collided, the stage was set for a tale of passion and betrayal unlike any other.

And as the clock struck the hour of reckoning, the players assembled, each with their own role to play in the drama that was about to unfold. For in the game of love and ambition, there are no winners, only survivors, clinging to the fragile threads of hope in a world consumed by shadows of deception.

PART I: EMBERS

CHAPTER I

SOLOMON

Solomon Pierce stood outside the grand wedding hall, his heart pounding in his chest. The early summer evening cast a golden glow over the manicured gardens, but Solomon barely noticed the beauty around him. His mind was a whirlpool of emotions—love, jealousy, fear. Autumn Evans, his best friend since childhood, was about to marry a man Solomon knew she shouldn't. Sylas Wilson was not the right man for her; Solomon was sure of it.

Autumn had always been the light of his life. Growing up together, they had shared everything—dreams, secrets, and countless moments of joy. Solomon had fallen in love with her somewhere along the way, but he had never found the courage to tell her. He feared ruining their friendship, feared losing her if she didn't feel the same. So he had kept his feelings to himself, content to be her confidant and closest friend.

But today, as he watched her prepare to marry another man, the weight of his silence felt unbearable. He had to do something, say something, before it was too late. Solomon had seen enough to suspect that Sylas was cheating on Autumn. He had no solid proof, just glimpses and whispers, but his gut told him that Sylas was hiding something. And Solomon's gut was rarely wrong.

The wedding rehearsal had been a tense affair. Solomon had tried to talk to Autumn, to warn her about Sylas, but she had brushed him off, too caught up in the whirlwind of wedding preparations. They had argued, their voices rising in the quiet of the empty hall.

"Autumn, please, listen to me," Solomon had pleaded, his voice tinged with desperation. "I don't trust Sylas. There's something off about him. I've seen things..."

Autumn had turned on him, her eyes flashing with anger. "Solomon, stop it! You're just jealous. Sylas is a good man, and he loves me. Why can't you be happy for me?"

"Because I care about you!" Solomon had shot back, his frustration boiling over. "I care about you more than you know. And I can't stand by and watch you make a mistake."

Autumn had stared at him, her expression softening for a moment. But then she had shaken her head, the anger returning. "This is my life, Solomon. My decision. Please, just support me. Be my friend."

The words had cut deep, but Solomon had nodded, forcing a smile. "Okay, Autumn. I'll be there for you."

But as he stood there now, watching guests arrive and the final preparations being made, he knew he couldn't let it go. He had to try one more time, had to make her see the truth. Taking a deep breath, he made his way into the hall, scanning the crowd for Autumn. He found her near the back, adjusting her veil and laughing with her sister, Audrey. She looked radiant, her happiness evident. It made Solomon's heart ache. He approached her, steeling himself for what he had to do.

"Autumn," he called softly, and she turned, her smile faltering when she saw the seriousness in his eyes. "Solomon, what is it?" she asked, a hint of impatience in her voice.

"Can we talk? Privately?" he asked, glancing at Audrey, who raised an eyebrow but said nothing. Autumn sighed but nodded. "Fine. Let's go to the garden."

They walked in silence to a secluded corner of the garden, away from the prying eyes of guests. Autumn crossed her arms, waiting for Solomon to speak.

"Autumn, I know you don't want to hear this, but I have to say it," Solomon began, his voice shaking slightly. "I love you. I've loved you for as long as I can remember. And I can't stand the thought of you marrying someone who doesn't deserve you."

Autumn's eyes widened in shock. "Solomon, I... I don't know what to say."

"Just listen," Solomon said quickly, before she could interrupt. "I have no solid proof, but I've seen Sylas with another woman. I think he's cheating on you. I can't prove it, but my gut tells me something is very wrong."

Autumn's face hardened. "You're wrong, Solomon. Sylas loves me. You're just jealous and trying to sabotage my happiness."

"No, Autumn, I'm trying to protect you!" Solomon insisted, his frustration mounting. "I care about you too much to see you get hurt."

She shook her head, tears brimming in her eyes. "You've already hurt me, Solomon. You couldn't just be happy for me, could you? You had to ruin everything."

Solomon reached out to touch her arm, but she stepped back, shaking her head. "I can't do this right now. The wedding is about to start. Please, just go."

"Autumn, please," Solomon whispered, but she had already turned away, walking back toward the hall.

Solomon stood there, his heart breaking. He had tried, but it hadn't been enough. Autumn was walking into a trap, and there was nothing he could do to stop it. He took a deep breath, trying to steady himself. He had to figure out what to do next.

As he made his way back toward the hall, he saw Sylas standing by the entrance, talking to a group of guests. Sylas's eyes met Solomon's, and for a moment, Solomon saw something dark and menacing in his gaze. It sent a chill down his spine.

Determined, Solomon decided to confront Sylas one last time. He couldn't let this go without a fight. Approaching Sylas, he squared his shoulders and took a deep breath.

"Sylas, we need to talk," Solomon said, his voice firm.
Sylas raised an eyebrow, his smile never faltering. "Of course, Solomon. What seems to be the problem?"
"Not here," Solomon muttered, glancing at the guests.

"Somewhere private."

Sylas nodded, his eyes narrowing slightly. "Lead the way."

Solomon led Sylas to the same secluded spot in the garden where he had spoken to Autumn. He turned to face Sylas, his heart pounding.

"Sylas, I know what you're doing," Solomon began, his voice low but steady. "I know you're cheating on Autumn. And I won't let you get away with it."

Sylas's smile disappeared, replaced by a cold, calculating expression. "You think you know me, Solomon? You think you can threaten me?"

"I'm not threatening you," Solomon replied, his hands shaking with anger. "I'm telling you to leave Autumn alone. She deserves better than you."

Sylas took a step closer, his eyes dark and dangerous. "You don't know anything about me or what I deserve. Autumn is mine, and there's nothing you can do about it."

Solomon clenched his fists, fighting the urge to punch Sylas. "I'm not afraid of you, Sylas. I'll do whatever it takes to protect Autumn."

Sylas laughed, a harsh, mocking sound. "You're a fool, Solomon. You can't protect her from me. And if you try, you'll regret it."

The threat hung in the air between them, heavy and ominous. Solomon knew he was in over his head, but he couldn't back down now. He had to find a way to expose Sylas, to save Autumn from making the biggest mistake of her life.

As he turned to leave, Sylas grabbed his arm, pulling him back. "This isn't over, Solomon. Stay out of my way, or you'll regret it."

Solomon yanked his arm free, glaring at Sylas. "We'll see about that."
He walked away, his mind racing. He needed a plan, needed to find a way to gather evidence against Sylas. But as he re-entered the wedding hall, he felt a growing sense of dread. Sylas was dangerous, and Solomon knew he was now a target.

He tried to shake off the fear, focusing on the task at hand. He had to find Autumn, had to make one last attempt to convince her. But as he moved through the crowd, he realized she was nowhere to be seen.

Panic surged through him as he searched the hall, asking guests if they had seen her. No one had. It was as if she had vanished.

His heart pounding, Solomon made his way to the office, hoping she might have gone there to clear her head. But as he opened the door, he was met with darkness. He stepped inside, calling her name.

"Autumn? Are you in here?"

There was no response. Solomon's anxiety grew, and he

moved further into the room, searching for any sign of her. As he reached the back of the office, he felt a sudden, sharp pain in his side.

He gasped, looking down to see blood seeping through his shirt. He turned, his vision blurring, to see Sylas standing behind him, a cold smile on his face.

"I warned you, Solomon," Sylas said softly, his voice dripping with malice. "You should have listened."

Solomon fell to his knees, the pain overwhelming. He tried to call for help, but his voice was weak, his strength fading. As darkness closed in around him, he thought of Autumn, of her smile, her laughter. He had failed her.

The last thing he saw was Sylas walking away, leaving him to die alone.

CHAPTER II

ELEANOR

Eleanor Evans stood at the back of the grand wedding hall, her lips pressed into a thin line of disapproval. The opulent decorations and lavish displays did nothing to ease the knot of disgust that twisted in her stomach. This marriage was an affront to everything she held dear—a union between her precious daughter, Autumn, and a middle-class man. It was simply unthinkable.

As Eleanor watched the guests mingling and the ceremony preparations underway, she couldn't help but feel a sense of unease. She had never approved of Sylas Wilson, the groom, from the moment Autumn had introduced him into their lives. He was beneath them in every way—socially, financially, even morally. Eleanor couldn't fathom why Autumn couldn't see that.

Autumn, her middle daughter, deserved nothing but the best. She was a shining star in Eleanor's eyes, a reflection of everything she had worked so hard to achieve. From the moment she was born, Eleanor had groomed Autumn to take her place in high society, to marry into wealth and power, to uphold the family name with grace and dignity. And now, all of that was in jeopardy because of this ill-conceived marriage.

As the ceremony began, Eleanor felt a surge of anger rise within her. She watched with narrowed eyes as Autumn walked down the aisle, her beautiful daughter, resplendent in her wedding gown. But instead of feeling pride, Eleanor felt only disgust. Disgust at the thought of Autumn being tied to a man like Sylas Wilson for the rest of her life. Disgust at the thought of her daughter throwing away everything she had worked so hard to achieve.

Throughout the ceremony, Eleanor's mind raced with thoughts of how to put a stop to this madness. She couldn't allow Autumn to go through with the marriage, couldn't allow her precious daughter to be dragged down by a man like Sylas. But try as she might, Eleanor couldn't think of a way to intervene without causing a scene. And so, she watched helplessly as the vows were exchanged, her heart heavy with despair.

After the ceremony, as the guests moved into the reception hall to celebrate, Eleanor found herself drawn to a quiet corner of the room. She needed a moment to collect her thoughts, to steel herself for the confrontation she knew was coming. She couldn't let this marriage stand, couldn't let her daughter be shackled to a man who was unworthy of her.

As she stood there, lost in thought, she was approached by Audrey, her eldest daughter. Audrey's expression was tense, her eyes troubled as she glanced around the room.

"Mother, we need to talk," Audrey said, her voice low but urgent.

Eleanor raised an eyebrow, her gaze sharp. "What is it, Audrey? Can't you see I'm busy?""It's about Autumn," Audrey replied, her tone brimming with concern. "She's not happy, Mother. She's making a mistake, marrying Sylas. We have to do something."

Eleanor's eyes narrowed, her anger flaring. "Of course she's not happy, Audrey. How could she be, marrying a man like Sylas? But there's nothing we can do about it now. The deed is done."

"But Mother, we can't just stand by and let this happen," Audrey insisted, her voice pleading. "We have to stop the wedding. We have to save Autumn from a lifetime of misery."

Eleanor shook her head, her lips pressed into a thin line. "And how do you propose we do that, Audrey? The guests are already here, the ceremony is over. It's too late."

"We have to try, Mother," Audrey urged, her eyes pleading. "For Autumn's sake. We can't let her make the biggest mistake of her life."

Eleanor hesitated, torn between her desire to protect her daughter and her fear of causing a scandal. But in the end, her maternal instinct won out. She couldn't let Autumn go through with this marriage, couldn't let her precious daughter be sacrificed on the altar of social propriety.

"Alright, Audrey," Eleanor said finally, her voice resolute. "We'll stop the wedding. Whatever it takes."

With that, Eleanor and Audrey sprang into action, determined to put an end to the travesty unfolding before them. They approached the bride's suite, where Autumn was preparing for the reception, and knocked on the door, their hearts pounding with anticipation.

"Autumn, darling, it's Mother," Eleanor called, her voice urgent. "We need to talk."

As the door swung open and they stepped inside, Eleanor knew that this was their last chance to save her daughter from a lifetime of misery. And she would do whatever it took to make sure that Autumn got the happy ending she deserved.

CHAPTER III

AISHA AND AMEEN

Aisha and Ameen Wilson stood together at the entrance of the grand wedding hall, greeting the arriving guests with warm smiles and firm handshakes. It was a perfect summer evening, and the golden light of the setting sun cast a warm glow over the festivities. They were beaming with pride and joy, thrilled to see their beloved son, Sylas, marrying into such a prestigious family.

For Aisha and Ameen, this wedding was not just a union of two people but a culmination of their efforts to ensure Sylas's success and happiness. They had raised him with unconditional love, always believing in his potential and overlooking his faults. To them, he was a precious ball of sunshine who could do no wrong. Their faith in him was unshakeable, and tonight was a testament to their unwavering support.

As they mingled with the guests, Aisha's eyes sparkled with excitement. "Oh, Ameen, can you believe it? Our Sylas is finally getting married. And to such a lovely girl, too. Autumn is perfect for him."

Ameen nodded, his chest swelling with pride. "Yes, she is. Sylas has always had a good head on his shoulders. He knows what's best for him. I'm sure their marriage will be a happy one."

They continued to greet guests, their smiles never

wavering. To them, the world was a place where everything was as it should be, and their son was the shining example of success and happiness.

Inside the hall, the atmosphere was electric with anticipation. The decorations were elegant, the flowers meticulously arranged, and the guests chattered excitedly, awaiting the ceremony. Aisha and Ameen took their seats near the front, eager to witness their son's special moment.

Aisha glanced around, her eyes searching for Sylas. She spotted him standing near the altar, talking to his best man, Callum. Her heart swelled with love and pride as she watched him. He looked handsome in his suit, confident and composed. She had always known he would achieve great things, and today was proof of that.

Ameen leaned over and whispered to her, "Look at him, Aisha. Our boy is all grown up. I knew he would make us proud."

Aisha nodded, tears of joy glistening in her eyes. "He has always been special, Ameen. From the moment he was born, I knew he was destined for greatness."

As the ceremony began, they watched with rapt attention, their hearts full of happiness. Autumn walked down the aisle, looking radiant in her wedding dress. Sylas's eyes were fixed on her, his expression unreadable but intense. Aisha and Ameen exchanged a glance, their faith in their son unwavering.The ceremony proceeded smoothly, the vows exchanged with heartfelt emotion. Aisha couldn't help but feel a pang of nostalgia as she remembered her own wedding day. She squeezed Ameen's hand, feeling grateful for the life they had built together and for the wonderful son they had raised.

After the ceremony, the reception was in full swing. Aisha and Ameen moved through the crowd, receiving congratulations and compliments on the beautiful wedding. They basked in the admiration, their pride in Sylas growing with each kind word.

"Aisha, Ameen, you must be so proud of Sylas," one guest said, raising a glass in their direction. "He's accomplished so much, and now he's married into such a wonderful family."

Aisha beamed. "Thank you. We are incredibly proud of him. He's worked hard to get where he is, and we couldn't be happier for him and Autumn."

Another guest chimed in, "You've raised a fine young man. He's always been so charming and successful. I'm sure he and Autumn will have a wonderful life together."

Ameen nodded in agreement, his smile never faltering. "Thank you. We've always believed in Sylas, and we know he will continue to make us proud."

As the evening wore on, Aisha and Ameen continued to mingle with the guests, their faith in Sylas shining brightly. They were oblivious to the darker undercurrents of the evening, the whispered conversations, and the concerned looks exchanged among some of the guests. To them, everything was perfect.

It wasn't until much later in the evening that Aisha noticed something amiss. She saw Autumn's mother, Eleanor, speaking with a sense of urgency to Audrey. Their faces were tense, their expressions worried. Aisha's brow furrowed in concern, and she nudged Ameen.

"Ameen, look. Something's going on with Eleanor and Audrey. They look upset."

Ameen followed her gaze and frowned. "I wonder what's happening. Maybe we should go over and see if everything is alright."

As they made their way toward Eleanor and Audrey, Aisha felt a knot of worry forming in her stomach. She had always trusted that everything would work out for the best, but seeing the distress on their faces made her uneasy.

"Is everything alright?" Aisha asked gently as they approached.

Eleanor looked up, her face pale and strained. "There's been a bit of a situation," she said, her voice tight. "Autumn is feeling unwell. She's in the bridal suite, resting."

Aisha's concern deepened. "Oh dear, I hope she's okay. Is there anything we can do to help?"
Audrey shook her head. "No, thank you, Aisha. We're just making sure she's comfortable. It's been a long and stressful day for her."

Ameen placed a comforting hand on Aisha's shoulder. "I'm

sure she'll be fine, Aisha. It's probably just nerves and exhaustion."

Aisha nodded, though her worry didn't abate. "If there's anything we can do, please let us know. We want to make sure Autumn is alright."

As they walked back to their seats, Aisha couldn't shake the feeling that something was wrong. She glanced over at Sylas, who was still mingling with guests, his expression calm and collected. Her heart ached with worry for Autumn, but she reminded herself that Sylas would take care of her. He had always been so capable, so reliable.

The evening continued, and Aisha and Ameen tried to enjoy the festivities, but the shadow of concern lingered over them. They kept a watchful eye on Sylas and the guests, hoping for any sign that Autumn was feeling better.

Finally, as the night drew to a close, Sylas approached them. His expression was composed, but Aisha could see a hint of strain in his eyes.

"Mom, Dad, I just wanted to thank you for everything," Sylas said, his voice warm but tinged with an undercurrent of tension. "Tonight has been wonderful, and I'm grateful for all your support."

Aisha reached out and hugged him tightly. "We're so proud of you, Sylas. We love you so much."

Ameen clapped Sylas on the back, his smile genuine. "You've made us incredibly proud, son. We know you and

Autumn will have a wonderful life together."

Sylas nodded, his smile a bit strained. "Thank you. It means a lot to me."

As they said their goodbyes and prepared to leave, Aisha couldn't shake the feeling of unease. She hoped that whatever had happened with Autumn was just a minor setback and that everything would be alright in the end.

As they drove home, Aisha looked out the window, her mind racing with thoughts of the evening. She trusted Sylas implicitly, but she couldn't ignore the nagging worry in the back of her mind. She hoped that their precious ball of sunshine would continue to shine brightly and that any clouds on the horizon would quickly dissipate.

Ameen reached over and squeezed her hand, offering silent comfort. "It's been a long day, Aisha. Try not to worry too much. Everything will be fine."Aisha nodded, though the worry remained. "I know, Ameen. I just want Sylas and Autumn to be happy."

CHAPTER IV

AUTUMN

Autumn Evans stood in front of the ornate mirror, her reflection a haunting reminder of the life she was about to be thrust into. Her wedding gown, a vision of white silk and lace, clung to her slender frame, masking the turmoil that churned within her heart.

As the middle sister of three, Autumn had always felt the weight of responsibility resting heavily upon her shoulders. Her father's untimely death before she was born had cast a shadow over her childhood, leaving her to navigate the complexities of life without his guiding hand.

And now, as she prepared to walk down the aisle, Autumn couldn't shake the sense of sadness that enveloped her like a suffocating cloak. This marriage was not of her choosing—it was a transaction, a business deal brokered by her mother in pursuit of wealth and status.

She cast a glance at the wedding ring sitting on the dressing table—a symbol of the life that awaited her, a life devoid of love and passion. Her best friend, Solomon, had warned her of the dangers of marrying for convenience, but Autumn had brushed aside his concerns, clinging to the hope that she could find happiness in spite of the circumstances.

But as she recalled their heated argument after the wedding rehearsal, a pang of guilt stabbed at her heart. Solomon had been right all along, and now she was paying the price for her stubbornness.

As she made her way to the grand ballroom, Autumn's steps faltered, her mind consumed by thoughts of what could have been. But before she could dwell on her regrets, a cry rang out from the crowd—a cry that sent a chill down her spine.

Her best friend was missing.

Panic gripped Autumn's heart as she searched the room frantically, her eyes darting from face to face in search of a familiar figure. But Solomon was nowhere to be found, and a sense of foreboding settled over her like a shroud.

But for Autumn, the news brought with it a sense of profound sadness—a sadness that threatened to consume her whole. Solomon had been more than just a friend; he had been her confidante, her protector, her rock in times of need.

And now he was gone, his life snuffed out in a cruel twist of fate.

As Autumn stood in the empty ballroom, her heart heavy with grief, she knew that her life would never be the same. The dreams of happiness and fulfillment she had harbored were nothing more than illusions, shattered by the harsh realities of the world.

But even in the depths of her despair, a glimmer of hope flickered in the darkness—a hope that one day, she would find the courage to forge her own path, to break free from the chains that bound her to a life she never wanted.

And as she wiped away her tears and faced the uncertain future that lay ahead, Autumn Evans vowed to honor Solomon's memory by living a life true to herself—a life filled with love, and laughter, and the promise of a brighter tomorrow.

Autumn couldn't help but feel a pang of regret as she recalled the events leading up to the wedding. Her argument with Solomon had weighed heavily on her mind, their words echoing in her ears like a relentless refrain.

She had been so caught up in the whirlwind of preparations, so focused on fulfilling her mother's expectations, that she had failed to see the pain in Solomon's eyes—the pain of unrequited love, of a friendship tested to its breaking point.

And now, as she stood on the precipice of a future she had never wanted, Autumn couldn't help but wonder if things could have been different—if she could have found the courage to follow her heart, to defy convention and embrace the possibility of a life worth living.

But as the memories threatened to overwhelm her, Autumn forced herself to push them aside. There was no turning back now, no undoing the choices that had brought her to this moment.

All she could do was face the future head-on, with all the strength and resilience she could muster. And as she took a deep breath and prepared to step out into the unknown,

Autumn knew that whatever lay ahead, she would face it with courage and determination—a determination to forge her own path, to reclaim control of her destiny, and to find the happiness she so desperately craved.

CHAPTER V

SYLAS

Sylas Wilson, a man of middle-class origins but with aspirations as lofty as the grand chandeliers adorning the Evans estate, stood at the threshold of the ballroom. His gaze swept across the opulent surroundings, the soft glow of candlelight casting an ethereal glow over the assembled guests. Tonight was not merely a wedding—it was a stage upon which Sylas would cement his place among the city's elite.

Despite his humble beginnings, Sylas had forged a path to success with single-minded determination. His business empire, once a mere fledgling venture, now stood as a testament to his ambition and cunning.
But beneath the facade of affable charm lay a darker truth—a sadistic streak that reveled in the thrill of manipulation and control.

As he moved through the crowd, exchanging pleasantries and feigned camaraderie, Sylas's mind drifted to the woman who waited for him at the altar—Autumn Evans, the bride whose hand he would soon possess. Their union was not one of love, but of convenience—a strategic alliance forged in the fires of ambition.

Beside him, Audrey Evans, Autumn's older sister and Sylas's closest confidante, offered a reassuring smile. They shared a bond forged in the crucible of shared ambition, a partnership built on mutual benefit and ruthless pragmatism.

But as the festivities reached their peak, a shrill ringtone pierced the air, cutting through the veneer of celebration like a knife. Sylas's hand tightened around his phone as he answered the call, his heart sinking with dread at the voice on the other end.

The police department—calling to interrupt the wedding with news that threatened to unravel everything Sylas had worked so tirelessly to achieve.

As he listened to the voice on the line, a cold knot of fear coiled in the pit of Sylas's stomach. His carefully constructed world was about to come crashing down, and there was nothing he could do to stop it.

But Sylas was not one to cower in the face of adversity. With a steely resolve, he steeled himself for the battle ahead—a battle that would test the limits of his ambition and the depths of his depravity.

And as he squared his shoulders and prepared to face the storm that loomed on the horizon, Sylas knew that whatever the future held, he would meet it head-on, with all the cunning and ruthlessness at his disposal.

Sylas glanced over at Autumn, who was chatting animatedly with some of the guests. She looked radiant, her smile lighting up the room, and for a brief moment, a pang of guilt stabbed at his heart. But he quicklypushed the feeling aside. This marriage was necessary—for business, for power, for everything he had worked so hard to achieve.

Audrey sidled up to him, her gaze sharp and calculating. "Everything alright, Sylas?"

Sylas forced a smile, though it felt strained on his lips. "Of course, Audrey. Just a minor hiccup. Nothing to worry about."

But even as he spoke the words, doubts gnawed at the edges of his mind. The police department's call was more than just a minor inconvenience—it was a harbinger of chaos, a sign that his carefully crafted plans were about to unravel.

As Sylas scanned the room, his eyes fell on Scarlet, his secret girlfriend and accomplice in his darkest deeds. She stood at the edge of the dance floor, her eyes burning with a fierce intensity that sent a shiver down his spine. They shared a silent exchange, a wordless communication that spoke volumes of the dangers that lurked beneath the surface of their seemingly perfect facade.

But before Sylas could dwell on the implications of their shared secrets, a commotion erupted at the back of the ballroom. He turned to see Raven, his loyal secretary, rushing towards him with a look of panic in her eyes.

"Sylas," she gasped, her breath coming in short, ragged bursts. "There's been an incident. You need to come with me."

Sylas's heart skipped a beat at the urgency in her voice. Without a second thought, he followed her out of the ballroom, leaving behind the glittering facade of the wedding celebration for the cold, harsh reality that awaited him outside.

As they hurried down the dimly lit corridor, Raven filled him in on the details—Solomon Pierce, Autumn's best friend, was dead. Murdered, according to the majority of the people at the wedding..

Sylas's mind raced as he tried to process the implications of the news. Solomon's death was more than just a tragedy—it was a threat to everything he had worked so hard to achieve. And as he stepped out into the night, the chill of uncertainty gripped him like a vice, squeezing the breath from his lungs and filling him with a sense of dread unlike anything he had ever known.

But Sylas was not one to back down from a challenge. With steely determination, he squared his shoulders and prepared to face whatever lay ahead—no matter the cost.

And as he ventured out into the darkness, leaving behind the glittering facade of the wedding celebration, Sylas Wilson knew that the true test of his ambition had only just begun.

CHAPTER VI

ASHLEY

She watched as the bride wed her handsome groom in peace. I pity the girl. She looked at the groom with his pretty little face and mouth that spoke lies. The young bride shyly approached her soon to be
mother-in-law to speak about her new life with her groom and what he expects of her. She looked at the groom once more. He was having small talk with his best man. "Most likely he shall be speaking of gold. I shouldn't be surprised if he has another business plan in mind" . It was true. The man had an itch for more gold. Every second of his life was spent earning gold, it seemed. Today he had a particularly grisly smile. In all the time she had seen him, he never smiled like this. Until yesterday. When she saw him reading of the deaths of several men near the western point of the English Channel. He had that same smile. That sneer of sorts. Something was off.

The bride came running to her asking if she had seen her best friend. "No dear, I'm sorry. I haven't seen him since last night" she said. The bride sprinted away to the next guest. But Ashley had her suspicions. She felt that the groom had something to do with it. The groom's brother was also behaving queerly. He was standing outside the hall. The man was accustomed to being isolated, from what she observed. He would always stand away from the crowd when he had done his part during the wedding rehearsal. Today seemed to be the same. He was minding his own business, whistling and drinking his wine. She didn't mind him. His presence just made her feel uneasy about the events to come.

A feast was to take place in honor of the wedding. The groom's brother didn't attend it as was expected of him. He just stood there, the fool. How could one disgrace such an occasion with no remorse, she never knew. The man looked quite ugly. He was unshaven, with hair all over his face. He had a lanky figure, all bent out of shape. His brother was much more comely. His jade eyes and pale face gave her the impression of a prince. His blond hair also commented on his fortunes.

And his fortunes were many indeed. His coffers were always filled with gold. He would never just convert it to cash. He'd wait till the rates reached extreme heights before cashing in his whole vault. That's how he'd gotten so rich over the years. "Or so he says" she thought. She always wondered how he got the money to start his first gold business, all the way in Africa. "It must have cost quite a lot, considering how much he got". It was true. He had earned millions in the first week of the operation. His parents hadn't funded the operation. And his inheritance wasn't even close to the amount needed for such an endeavor. She suspected foul play was involved.

It simply wasn't possible. He couldn't spend so much without some form of earning money beforehand. Unless he scammed someone. He had launched the South Africa Gold scheme mere weeks after he had turned 18. Shiploads of miners had been sent off to the continent and had given him a plentiful amount of gold just days into the inauguration. How they were paid for such good work was beyond her. She quietly feasted on some chicken while her older sister babbled away to her husband. "The poor man seems to have had enough already," she mused, watching them. Her sister was always the chatty kind.The bridesmaids were perfect emulations of her as well. Whispering amongst themselves like little girls about who knows what. She didn't mind it as long as the subject of their gossiping concerned her. The chicken was quite good, she felt. For such a wedding, it would serve to have slightly more though. Either way, food was food.

She wrapped up her meal and washed it down with some french wine. French gold, rather. The whole wedding was gold. But the groom wanted more. Her family's wealth was nearly double that of the groom's, amassed from generations of men involved in all sorts of trades, from spices to silk to oil, which was their primary product as of today. The family owned at least 5 oil rigs in Saudi Arabia alone, along with some on the gulf coast. The black gold they earned would soon turn yellow and fill their coffers. Of which they had plenty. Plenty of coffers for plenty of gold. Her family wasn't much like that of the groom's. Instead of having multiple businesses in different sectors, they had one large business in the oil industry. The business had started in the '40s when the demand for oil was high for redevelopment following the second world war. The oil sold well, until the British were thrown out of the middle east. So they started using sea rigs, although they weren't as profitable as the ones they had on the gulf, it sufficed. That was until the middle east started allowing the US to purchase their oil. Her grandfather jumped at the opportunity and immediately purchased five of the oil rigs in the nation so they would reap the benefits. And with those benefits they built their own rigs along the gulf coast.

Her own life had been spent learning how to convince a man to fund them. All sorts of quirks and tricks to help her out. She had convinced a few sponsors to help them out after what happened in 2008. She got a few donors in hand, and they did give them significant amounts of money, yet it was her older sisters who got all the attention even though she contributed the most. In fact, half of the donors they were credited for were actually suggested and given by her.

She honestly didn't care. The buffoons she called sisters were both married off to rich handsome husbands with rich handsome lands so they wouldn't even have to do a minute of work for the rest of their lives. "Until their husbands get arrested, that is' '. Both her sisters were married to scheming frauds who had risen to power in somewhat questionable ways. Although they did it all under the name of businesses, she already saw through her oldest sister's husband when she found him talking to known gangsters regarding the sale of opium. As for this one, she was yet to see what he would come up with. Their parents, of course, were ignorant donkeys who didn't realise that their sons were bloody criminals for 10 years now.

It really didn't matter though. As long as she was married to someone at least half decent she was fine with it, although she would prefer to remain unmarried for the rest of her life. Either way she had no gold, because her fat headed sisters had gotten it all. What'd she get? One oil rig off the gulf coast that had been shut down for years. Her parents had said that it was "Quite a lot as it is, you don't need more than that". She visited the rig herself, and saw that it was just a barge with a tank and a pipe going down from it with some controls along with a small control tower and a meagre staff of three workers from Africa.

She watched with a sense of detachment as the bride exchanged vows with her handsome groom, a pang of pity coursing through her. The girl was oblivious, blissfully unaware of the deceit lurking beneath her groom's charming facade. Ashley's gaze lingered on the groom, his features adorned with a grin that sentshivers down her spine. It was a grin she had seen before, one that spoke of sinister intentions veiled beneath a veneer of affability.

As the bride timidly approached her soon-to-be mother-in-law, Ashley couldn't help but feel a sense of foreboding. She knew all too well what was expected of the young bride, the sacrifices she would be forced to make in the name of her groom's insatiable greed.

Her suspicions only deepened when the bride frantically sought her missing best friend. Ashley feigned ignorance, but she couldn't shake the feeling that the groom was somehow involved. And his brother, with his aloof demeanor and unnerving presence, only added to her unease.

The lavish feast that followed was a testament to the groom's ostentatious display of wealth. His brother's absence only served to highlight the discord within the family, a rift born out of greed and deception.
Ashley observed the guests with a critical eye, her mind reeling with thoughts of the groom's dubious business dealings and his family's complicity in his schemes.

Her thoughts drifted to her own family's wealth, amassed through generations of exploitation and manipulation. Unlike the groom's family, who flaunted their wealth with reckless abandon, Ashley's family preferred to operate in the shadows, their true motives obscured by a veil of respectability.

Her mind wandered back to her childhood, spent navigating the treacherous waters of her family's ambitions. She had learned early on the art of manipulation, the subtle nuances of persuasion that had allowed her to secure funding for their ventures. But despite her efforts, she remained overshadowed by her older sisters, their marriages to wealthy scoundrels a testament to their willingness to sacrifice morality for material gain.

Yet Ashley harboured no illusions about her family's true nature. Behind their façade of respectability lurked a darkness that she could no longer ignore. Her sisters' husbands were not the upstanding gentlemen they pretended to be, their wealth built on a foundation of deceit and corruption.

But Ashley had no desire to follow in their footsteps. She had seen firsthand the cost of their ambition, the toll it had taken on their souls. She would rather remain unmarried than sacrifice her principles for the sake of wealth and status.

As she finished her meal and washed it down with a sip of wine, Ashley felt a sense of resignation wash over her. She may not have the wealth or status of her sisters, but she had something far more valuable: her integrity. And in a world consumed by greed and deceit, that was a currency worth more than gold.

CHAPTER VII

CALLUM

Callum stood beside Sylas, his best man duties weighing heavily on his shoulders. The polished smile he wore belied the uncertainty churning within him. He and Sylas had been more than friends—they were former dorm mates, brothers in arms who had weathered the storms of university life together.

Sylas had been a godsend during Callum's darkest days, swooping in like a guardian angel to rescue him from the brink of financial ruin. Callum owed him everything, and he idolized the groom with a fervor bordering on worship.

In Callum's eyes, Sylas could do no wrong. His charm, his charisma, his unwavering confidence—they were qualities to be admired, emulated, worshiped. And so, when Sylas asked for his help, Callum had jumped at the chance, no questions asked.

But as the wedding day unfolded, a sense of unease gnawed at the edges of Callum's mind. There were whispers, rumors, hints of something darker lurking beneath the surface of Sylas's perfect facade. But Callum brushed them aside, unwilling to entertain the notion that his idol could be anything less than perfect.

As the ceremony progressed, Callum's admiration for Sylas only grew. The groom's poise and confidence were on full display, captivating the audience with every word he spoke.

Callum watched in awe, his heart swelling with pride at the thought of being associated with such a remarkable man.

But amidst the celebrations, a shadow loomed—a shadow that threatened to shatter the illusion of perfection that surrounded Sylas. It started with a whispered rumor, a fleeting glance exchanged between guests. Callum's stomach churned with unease as he struggled to reconcile the image of his idol with the whispers of doubt that echoed in the back of his mind.

And then, just as the vows were about to be exchanged, the call came—a call that sent shockwaves rippling through the crowd, disrupting the festivities with its grim tidings.

Solomon Pierce, Autumn's best friend, was dead.

The news struck Callum like a physical blow, his mind reeling with disbelief. Solomon had been a constant presence in Autumn's life, a friend and confidant whose absence would be keenly felt. And now, his life had been cut short in a senseless act of violence, leaving behind a void that could never be filled.

But amidst the chaos and confusion that followed, Callum's thoughts turned to Sylas. His idol, his hero, his guardian angel—what role had he played in this tragedy? The whispers grew louder, the doubts more insistent, until Callum could no longer ignore the nagging voice of suspicion that tugged at the corners of his mind.
And yet, even as doubt gnawed at his conscience, Callum found himself unable to abandon his allegiance to Sylas. The man who had saved him, who had lifted him up from

the depths of despair—he couldn't bear to believe that Sylas was anything less than the paragon of virtue he had always imagined him to be.

And so, with a heavy heart and a sense of duty weighing him down, Callum stood by Sylas's side, ready to do whatever it took to protect the man he admired above all others.

As the hours stretched into eternity, Callum found himself lost in a whirlwind of emotions. Guilt gnawed at him, a constant reminder of the doubts that lingered in the back of his mind. Had he been too quick to dismiss the whispers of suspicion? Too eager to defend his idol against the accusations that threatened to tear his perfect world apart?

But try as he might, Callum couldn't shake the feeling that something was amiss. Solomon's death had cast a pall over the wedding, transforming what should have been a joyous occasion into a somber affair tinged with grief and regret.

As the guests drifted away, their voices hushed in solemn reflection, Callum found himself alone with his thoughts. He replayed the events of the day in his mind, searching for answers that remained frustratingly out of reach.

And then, in the silence of the empty ballroom, a flicker of doubt ignited within him—a spark of realization that threatened to consume him whole.

Sylas Wilson, his idol, his hero, his guardian angel—was not the man he thought he was.

Callum's heart raced as he grappled with the implications of his revelation. The man he had admired, trusted, worshipped—was he capable of such darkness? Such deceit?

As the weight of his realization settled over him, Callum felt a sense of betrayal unlike anything he had ever known. He had placed his faith in Sylas without question, blindly following him down a path that now seemed fraught with danger.

But even as doubt gnawed at his conscience, Callum knew that he couldn't turn back. He had made a choice, and now he had to live with the consequences—whatever they may be.

He replayed the events of the day in his mind, scrutinizing every interaction, every glance exchanged between Sylas and Solomon. Had there been a hint of malice in Sylas's eyes? A trace of guilt in his smile?

The questions swirled around in Callum's mind, taunting him with their elusive answers. He wanted to believe in Sylas—to cling to the image of the man who had saved him from ruin. But the nagging doubts refused to be silenced, growing louder with each passing moment.As the sun dipped below the horizon and the stars emerged like silent sentinels in the night sky, Callum found himself grappling with a decision that would shape the course of his future. Should he confront Sylas, demand answers to the questions that plagued his mind? Or should he remain silent, burying his doubts beneath a facade of loyalty and obedience?

The choice weighed heavily on Callum's shoulders, a burden too great to bear alone. He longed for the clarity that had eluded him, the certainty that had once filled his heart with unwavering devotion. But now, all he felt was a gnawing sense of unease—a creeping suspicion that threatened to consume him whole.

As the hours stretched on, Callum wrestled with his conscience, torn between loyalty to his friend and the truth that beckoned from the shadows. He knew that whatever path he chose, there would be consequences—consequences that could not be undone.

And so, with a heavy heart and a sense of resignation, Callum made his decision. He would confront Sylas, demand the truth that had eluded him for so long. He could no longer bear to live in ignorance, to blindly follow a man whose true nature remained shrouded in darkness.

As dawn broke and the first light of morning filtered through the curtains, Callum squared his shoulders and prepared to face the truth—whatever it may be.

The journey ahead would be fraught with peril, fraught with uncertainty. But Callum knew that he could no longer turn a blind eye to the doubts that tormented him. He owed it to himself, to Solomon, to Autumn—to uncover the truth, no matter the cost.

And so, with resolve burning in his heart, Callum set out to confront Sylas—to peel back the layers of deception and uncover the darkness that lurked beneath the surface of his perfect facade.

For better or for worse, the truth awaited, and Callum was determined to face it head-on.

CHAPTER VIII

RAVEN

Raven White stood at her usual post near the back of the opulent wedding hall, eyes darting across the room as she took in the scene. The wedding of Sylas Wilson and Autumn Evans was in full swing, a lavish affair that spoke to wealth and careful planning. But Raven, Sylas's secretary, was far from enjoying the spectacle. A heavy knot of fear had settled in her stomach, tightening with each passing moment.

She knew everything about Sylas—the good, the bad, and the very ugly. As his secretary, she had been privy to all his secrets, including his affair with Scarlet La Quelle. She had watched from the sidelines as Sylas spun a web of lies, deceiving his fiancée, Autumn, with practiced ease. And she had kept her mouth shut, terrified of losing her job and the stability it provided.

The ceremony had begun smoothly, the bride and groom exchanging vows under a canopy of white roses. Raven stood on the periphery, her mind racing. The knowledge of Sylas's infidelity weighed heavily on her conscience, but fear kept her silent. She had seen what happened to those who crossed Sylas—how their lives were systematically dismantled, their careers destroyed. Raven had no desire to become one of his casualties.

As the couple exchanged rings and sealed their vows with a kiss, Raven's anxiety reached a fever pitch. She glanced at Scarlet, who stood among the guests, her eyes filled with silent rage. It was a look Raven had come to recognize well. Scarlet despised this marriage, and the facade they all maintained felt like a charade that could crumble at any moment.

Raven tried to focus on her tasks, checking off items on her clipboard and ensuring everything ran smoothly. The reception was set to begin immediately after the ceremony, and she needed to ensure all preparations were perfect. But her hands trembled as she worked, the fear gnawing at her insides.

Just as the newlyweds and guests moved to the reception hall, Raven slipped away, needing a moment to collect herself. She headed toward the office, her safe haven amidst the chaos. But as she pushed open the door, she was met with a sight that froze her blood.

Solomon Pierce, Autumn's best friend, lay motionless on the floor, his body twisted in an unnatural position. Blood pooled around him, a stark contrast to the pristine white carpet. Raven's breath caught in her throat, a scream dying on her lips.

Panic surged through her, her mind racing as she tried to process what she was seeing. She had to do something—she had to call for help. With trembling hands, she reached for her phone, but as she dialed, she stopped. If she involved the police, Sylas would know it was her. She couldn't risk that.She took a deep breath, forcing herself to think. She needed to get out of there, to get as far away from this mess as possible. She quickly deleted the call from her phone's history, wiped her fingerprints from any surfaces she had touched, and left the office, her heart pounding in her chest.

Raven rejoined the reception, trying to act normal. The noise, the laughter, and the music felt surreal, like a twisted dream she couldn't wake up from. She spotted Sylas by the bar, his arm around Autumn, who was laughing at something he had said. The sight made her stomach churn.

Raven approached them, forcing a smile. "Everything alright here?" she asked, her voice remarkably steady.

"Just peachy," Sylas replied, his eyes scanning her face for any sign of distress. "Can you check on the arrangements for the departure? Make sure everything's perfect."

"Of course," Raven said, nodding. She turned to leave, but not before catching Scarlet's eye from across the room. The look they exchanged was brief but loaded with unspoken tension. Scarlet knew. She had to.

As Raven walked away, her mind was a whirlwind of thoughts. She needed to find a way out of this nightmare, but every path seemed fraught with danger. She couldn't go to the police; she had already reported the body anonymously, but revealing her identity now would link her directly to Sylas and his dark world. She couldn't confront Sylas; he was too powerful and too ruthless. She couldn't trust Scarlet; the woman was a wild card, driven by her own agenda.

Her only option was to find a way to protect herself while

gathering enough evidence to expose Sylas without putting herself in the line of fire. But how?

The clock was ticking. Each minute felt like an hour as Raven moved through the reception, her mind racing with potential plans. She discreetly checked her phone, making sure no one saw the anxiety that was practically radiating from her. She needed a plan, and she needed it fast.

She spotted Callum, Sylas's best man, laughing heartily with a group of groomsmen. Callum idolized Sylas, seeing him as an angel who could do no wrong. Raven knew that trying to convince Callum of Sylas's true nature would be futile. Instead, she needed to find a way to use Callum's naivety to her advantage.

Making her way to Callum, Raven forced a smile. "Hey, Callum, can I borrow you for a second? I need help with something in the office."

"Of course, Raven," Callum said, always eager to be of assistance. He followed her willingly, chatting about how perfect the day was going.

Once they were alone, Raven closed the office door behind them. She needed to tread carefully. "Callum, I found something...something terrible," she began, her voice shaking just enough to convey urgency without giving away her full fear.
Callum frowned, concern creasing his brow. "What is it, Raven?"

"It's Solomon," she whispered, her voice barely audible.

"He's...he's dead." Callum's face went white. "What How? Where?"

"In here," Raven gestured to the side room where Solomon's body lay. "I think someone might have...hurt him."

Callum's eyes widened, and he stepped back, clearly horrified. "We have to tell Sylas! He'll know what to do!"

"No!" Raven's voice was sharper than intended. She softened it immediately. "I mean, we can't. Not yet. We need to figure out what happened first. If we go to Sylas without any information, it could cause a panic."

Callum looked torn, his loyalty to Sylas battling with the horror of the situation. "What do we do, then?"

Raven thought quickly. "We need to secure the area and make sure no one else comes in here. Can you help me with that? We need to keep this quiet until we know more."

Callum nodded, albeit reluctantly. "Okay, Raven. I'll trust you on this."

As Callum went to secure the area, Raven's mind raced. She had bought herself a little time, but she needed a more permanent solution. She knew that Solomon's death would not go unnoticed for long. The moment someone else found the body, chaos would ensue.

All she had to do was make sure no one saw the body. She could make up a ruse. Yes, that would work. Solomon drank too much and started feeling dizzy so he went outside for a walk. Or maybe he went home because he had urgent business to take care of. But instead of any of that, she came up with what would otherwise have been the most likely possibility. The bride came running up to her that very moment.

"Have you seen Solomon? I haven't seen him since the wedding started. Where is he?!"

"Oh, yes. He told me he was going home because he was getting bored of the wedding processions.
Mumbled something about important business and finding out the truth."

"But what could be more important to him than my own wedding?!"

"You have a lot to learn, dear. A lot to learn indeed."

Saying that, she left, knowing that the dark truth would have to stay with her, and her alone.

CHAPTER IX

SCARLET

As Scarlet slipped into the shadows, her mind raced with thoughts of retribution. She would not let Sylas and Autumn get away with their betrayal—not if she had anything to say about it.

But as she plotted her revenge, a small voice whispered in the back of her mind—a voice that warned of the dangers that lay ahead. Scarlet pushed the voice aside, her rage burning brighter with each passing moment.

She would not be deterred. She would not be denied.

For Scarlet La Quelle, vengeance was a dish best served hot—like the flames of her burning fury.

As the guests began to disperse, Scarlet remained hidden in the shadows, her eyes never leaving the newlyweds. Sylas and Autumn moved through the crowd, their smiles radiant, their happiness palpable. But to Scarlet, their joy was nothing more than a cruel mockery—a slap in the face to everything she had sacrificed for them.

Her anger bubbled to the surface, threatening to boil over at any moment. But Scarlet forced herself to remain calm, to bide her time until the opportunity presented itself. She would have her revenge, but she had to be patient. She had to wait for the perfect moment to strike.

As the night wore on, Scarlet kept a watchful eye on Sylas and Autumn, searching for any sign of weakness, any hint of vulnerability. But try as she might, she could find no chink in their armor—no opportunity to exploit.

Frustration gnawed at her, fueling the flames of her rage until they threatened to consume her whole. But Scarlet refused to give in. She had come too far to let her emotions get the better of her now.

And then, just as she was about to give up hope, she saw it—a fleeting glance exchanged between Sylas and one of the waitstaff. It was a small, insignificant gesture, but to Scarlet, it was a revelation.

A plan began to form in her mind—a plan to exploit Sylas's weaknesses, to tear down the facade of perfection that he had spent so long building. It would be risky, dangerous even, but Scarlet knew that she had no other choice. She had to strike now, before it was too late.

With a renewed sense of purpose, Scarlet slipped through the crowd, her steps light and purposeful. She had a mission now—a mission to bring Sylas to his knees, to make him pay for the pain he had caused her.

And as she disappeared into the night, a smile played at the corners of her lips—a smile that promised retribution, a smile that promised justice.

For Scarlet La Quelle would have her revenge. And woe betide anyone who dared to stand in her way.

As Scarlet moved through the shadows, her mind raced

with possibilities. She knew she needed a plan, something clever and devastating that would strike at the heart of Sylas's carefully constructed world. And then, it came to her—a glimmer of an idea, a seed of revenge that took root in her mind and refused to let go.

She would expose Sylas's infidelity for all to see—to shatter the illusion of his perfect marriage and reveal the darkness lurking beneath the surface. But she would need help, someone on the inside who could provide her with the information she needed to bring Sylas down.

With determination burning in her veins, Scarlet set out to find her ally. She moved with purpose through the dimly lit corridors of the mansion, her steps quick and purposeful. She had no time to waste—every moment brought her one step closer to her goal.

And then, she saw him—a young waiter, his eyes darting nervously as he cleared away empty glasses from the tables. Scarlet approached him with a confidence she didn't feel, her heart pounding in her chest.

"Excuse me," she said, her voice low and urgent. "I need to speak with you."

The waiter looked up, his eyes widening in surprise at the sight of Scarlet's intense gaze. "Who are you?" he asked, his voice trembling slightly.

"I'm a friend," Scarlet replied, her tone leaving no room for argument. "And I need your help."

She quickly explained her plan to the waiter, laying out the details with precision and clarity. To her relief, he nodded eagerly, his fear giving way to a sense of determination.

"I'll do it," he said, his voice steady now. "I'll help you bring him down."

With her ally secured, Scarlet felt a surge of adrenaline course through her veins. She was one step closer to her goal, one step closer to tearing down the man who had betrayed her.

But she knew she couldn't act hastily. She needed to gather more information, to build her case against Sylas with care and precision. And so, she and the waiter set to work, gathering evidence and piecing together the puzzle of Sylas's deception.

As the night wore on, Scarlet's determination only grew stronger. She was unstoppable now, a force to be reckoned with—a woman on a mission to destroy the man who had wronged her.

Sometime later, Sylas walked towards her smirking.

"I know your plan." he said.
"What plan?"
"You're a journalist who specialises in crime. What should I expect?"
"Well, too late. I have it all over here." she pointed to her bag.
"Looks like it is. I suppose we should toast to your victory before my grand reveal, eh?"

"Alright. Nothing wrong in that I suppose."
"I'll treat you to a cup of some of my personal favourite wine. Here, have a swig." he pulled a bottle out of his pocket and served her a cup.

She drank. And she drank more. A few minutes later she was drunk. But then suddenly there was a sharp pain in her chest, as if it were heating up. Oh no. The last thing she saw was Sylas' unnaturally handsome face smiling down at her.

CHAPTER X

JORAH

He watched the wedding proceedings take place with a grin on his face. "Let's hope my brother and his bride remain together in the heavens" he mused. Thinking this, he went towards the drinks table and took a sip of wine. He tipped a bottle of Alcohol and allowed it to flow down onto the wedding hall's floor. As he exited the hall, he informed his brother's best man that he was going out for some fresh air. "The wedding hall is quite stuffy, I must say" said the timid lad. "I agree, boy. I suggest you remain here in the hall so as to not disappoint my dear brother. After all, I do not wish to see him saddened on his own wedding day".

Saying this, he exited the hall. "Ah yes, the beautiful night air. What could be better than this?" he thought to himself, relishing the cool breeze, knowing he would be forced into that forsaken hall once more. He watched as the bride and groom walked down the aisle together, to a thunderous applause from all the guests congratulating them on being wed. "I can hardly wait for my own wedding to take place" he mused. He was the younger of the two, obviously. His older brother had always overshadowed him. He would get everything. A good wife, the larger part of the inheritance, even his own mansion and plot to start his own business. And him? He got a measly ten percent of his father's money, a small little cottage for a house and a plot that used to be part of a garbage depot! And the worst of it all was that he was betrothed to some foolish whore from a brothel in the bad side of town! He was naturally quite jealous of his brother. But now he would get everything he wanted. He just had to wait.

The seconds ticked by as he watched the hustle and bustle of the festivities in the wedding hall. "My brother seems to be quite a celebrity I must say" he thought. He wondered if he would be as popular when he took over the company. He had always been overshadowed in his boyhood. Every child seemed to be better than him in something. When his parents commented on his apparent mediocrity as a boy he always brooded over some potential talents that would make him win his parents' pride and attention. He tried mnemonics; but when he memorized a deck of cards in front of his parents, some boy on the television memorized two. When he tried his hand at academics, his brother pointed out the singular B he had gotten on his report card, all the while gloating about his "perfect" report card. He knew that was fake. Nearly everything his brother had done was fake. He claimed to have started a small clothing business, but only Jorah knew that those clothes hid a truckload of drugs that his brother was selling in the black market. "I'll show these ignorant fools what a scumbag their so-called perfect son was. I'll make sure to expose every scandal he was part of. Get his partners arrested as well."

His brother had been engaging in questionable activities ever since he got out of school. "The world is mine for the taking" he would say. That seemed to have turned out well. He had taken the world. Or at least a good chunk of it to say the least. He had things going on across the English Channel, naturally. He had overheard conversations between his brother and some shady smuggler with a thick accent. He sounded french. His brother would later reveal that he was an illegal weapons dealer from Normandy. Another time he was found conversing with some Arab about an oil deal. That same Arab was caught a month later in Qatar selling oil to a shady company from the black market. THat shady company was his brother's, who promptly shut it down while telling their parents that the middle east was too dangerous tocontinue his operations there. The numbskulls believed that, of course. Their precious little son could be harmed. He, on the other hand, had nearly been kidnapped once when he was young and his parents shrugged it off as a small incident of bullying. They hadn't even tried to search for him. Instead, it was his teacher who found him surrounded by those thugs in the school courtyard.

He passed some time in this brooding. He thought over his plan again. In his head it sounded fairly simple. He would just have to figure out a way to burn the hall and then escape it. The hard part would be actually burning the hall. He would escape it alright, but not unscathed. He would most likely suffer some minor burns and injuries. Then he would feign grief for the dead guests of the wedding and make a public speech and whatnot. "The usual drama that follows such an influential person's death" he thought. He was collaborating with journalists and private detectives around the world to slowly uncover the scandals his brother was a part of. They had discovered quite a lot, although none of it was reported to local authorities. He didn't want his brother in jail. Either way he would just ask some acquaintance to pay his bail and he would be free to go. "Better to have him dead than have him getting out of jail every now and then while clearing his name. Saves the news some hassle." he realized. He would make sure that each journalist unveiled one scandal at a time over a period of a few months to ease the tension. He would also make sure to include his part in the research. Unlike his brother, who spent his time at lavish banquets and dinners while rolling out swathes of money to the people he hired, Jorah actually played a part in the work he wanted done. He had personally done some research and dug into his brother's computer and found some concrete evidence about the drug scandal as well as his oil and gold smuggling operations around the world. "My brother should protect his computer better" he reflected.

It had been quite easy to get into it, truly. "Will my brother ever learn the true value of things such as education?" he wondered. Considering how much value his brother had for money as well as his family, he doubted that he even cared about his education. He recalled once when he had asked his brother a question after he saw him drinking in a pub downtown. "Do you have a shred of honor?" he had asked. His brother responded by saying that there was no such businessman with this so-called "honor". "Honor is a thing of the past, little brother. Men don't need honor to prove their worth. In today's world, your worth is in your gold and cunning. It lies in your fame, not your oaths. Who cares if I'm drinking in some brothel downtown? I'm quite famous and run a successful business, that's what matters. Not honor." Well, his honor would soon be playing a major role in determining how people would see him after he died. And naturally that wouldn't end well, for his older brother. "Well, it's time," he thought.

A quarter of an hour's patient waiting led to nothing. Only an awful amount of rage and curses muttered from his mouth. So he did it himself. He walked toward the dining table and sat next to his dear brother. Then as he reached out for some gravy to add to his fish and chips, he knocked down a candelabra. He apologized for his folly and went to get the extinguisher.

Or so they thought. He exited the hall once more to get this so-called fire extinguisher and as soon as he stepped out of the hall, it burst into flames. He watched as they all screamed and writhed in pain from the flames of the candles. He heard screams and shouts and saw hands and arms rise out of the flames, groping for who knows what. He saw the bride and the groom struggling through the flames. The bride tripped and got consumed by the flames. The groom began to flee. But he was stopped by his brother."Where do you think you're going, my dear brother?" he asked. "Spare me Jorah! I'll give you anything, The mansion, the company, my wife, anything! Just don't kill me!"

"A man who is willing to sell his wife to save himself does not deserve to live". Saying this, he pulled out his knife and pointed it towards his brother. "This blade is the blade that will avenge all those you have wronged for your selfish desires, my dear brother. All those scams and gold and money, some of your partners barely escaped prison by the skin of their teeth. Some weren't so lucky. Others were as lucky as you are."

"Wh-What do you mean? What scams? I had nothing to do with the gold scandal I swear. They bribed me. Ransomed one of my very own school friends. I had no choice." he pleaded.

"Lies. Your life is a lie, my dear brother. Consider this a parting gift from me. Quite literally the only gift I will personally give you with my own heart. A wonderful one at that." he said.

"What d'you mean? Are you killing me? This is fratricide! You can't do this! I'm your brother, right?" the man wailed.

"Funny to see you acknowledge that after all these years. Well, yes, you are my brother, you see. It's just that you haven't fulfilled certain requirements of a brother. Firstly, you weren't the best person to look up to. All those scandals and lies aren't exactly pretty on their own, y'know. You dressed them up quite well, I must say."

"Jorah, I plead with you to have mercy. You can't do this. You're right. I've committed countless sins. But I can change that. Just let me live."

"You're mistaken, brother. I am giving you mercy, by killing you. So you don't have to rot in a prison cell for the rest of your days. Now, adios, my dear brother. I shall see you in the skies."

Saying that, he plunged the knife into his brother's heart.

"NOOOOOOOOOOOOOOOOOOOOOOOOOO" he shouted. And then his body fell. Down into the flames of death.

PART II - ASHES

CHAPTER XI

FENTON

Fenton Wilson, the carefree preteen son of Jorah Wilson, stood outside an average Manchester four-bedroom house on a cloudy afternoon. He had just arrived at his father's house to spend his annual holidays there. He set his suitcase down on the front porch and returned to pay the taxi driver waiting on the driveway. After the taxi pulled away, he went back to the front door and rang the doorbell. In barely ten seconds, the door swung open and his father welcomed him inside, "Fenton, dear, I missed you so much! Please follow me to my study. Give me your bag, I'll take it. "Sure, thank you," replied Fenton. After wiping his feet on the doormat, he followed his father inside.

"Fenton, take a seat! Tell me how it's been at St Bernard's!"

Fenton, glad to see his father after almost a year, took a seat while answering the question, "Well, Dad, it's been going good so far. But I keep feeling homesick. I just wish I could go back to studying in Manchester at a normal day school".

"Fenton, dear, I want the best for you. That's why I want you to study in one of the best boarding schools I can afford." Jorah's reply, however, was only part of the truth.

The complete reason was due to the wedding hall incident that had happened nearly fourteen years ago. Almost 26 months ago, Jorah, feeling guilty for murdering his family, had confessed his involvement in the Wedding hall incident at a nearby police station. However, Jorah was only sentenced to a few months of therapy due to mental stress. Sylas's lawyer, Joseph, came to know of this information and had begun to stalk Jorah. To avoid any chances of his son being harmed by Joseph, Jorah had enrolled Fenton in the St Bernard's boarding school far away in London, claiming it was for a better education. Of course, Fenton had believed this because, for all he knew, his uncle, Sylas, and grandparents, Aisha and Ameen, had died in a major road accident before he was born.

"Oh well, if you say so, Dad." Fenton sighed in disappointment.

"You sound exhausted, Fenton. Your travel must have been tiring," said Jorah, desperate for a change in topic. "Your room has been set up, and a delicious meal is waiting for you on the dining table. But first, go and get freshened up in the shower. After that, we can go for a walk, if you're ok."

"Sounds good Dad," the fatigued twelve-year-old replied as he rose from his chair.

CHAPTER XII

ANYA

Anya Wilson, the kind wife of Jorah Wilson, descended the staircase of the Manchester house. Anya couldn't meet her son the day before as she had gone to the doctor because she was feeling a bit ill. She entered the dining room and found that her son was already seated and had begun eating.

"Fenton, honey, I missed you so much! Tell me how it's been at school so far away from home!" greeted Anya as she hugged her son.

"Good morning mum! School is good in London, but I miss being with you and Dad." Fenton replied, joyful to see his mother.

Anya felt bad for her son. She knew that Fenton had been moved to another city to be protected, but the danger itself was caused by his father.

Anya took her seat and helped herself to some pancakes and Yorkshire pudding.

"Mum, where's dad?" Inquired the son.

"Oh Fenton, you know your father, he was caught up with some work and had to stay up late into the night. He wanted to sleep in this morning," explained Anya.

Fenton signed with disappointment. Anya felt bad hearing

her son's sigh.

Jorah Wilson hadn't slept until 2 AM because he had received yet another threatening Email from Joseph. Under normal circumstances, Jorah would have ignored the Email. This time, however, since his son was at home, Jorah had called his lawyer, Roy, and had informed him of the matter. Roy and Jorah had stayed up late into the night to discuss this matter.

"Fenton, what would you like to do on the first day of your holidays?" asked Anya, in an attempt to brighten her son's mood.

Fenton looked up at his mother "Oh, I don't know mum. I was hoping I could visit some of my old friends today. I really miss them. I think I'll go and play with Charlie as well."

"Ok, that sounds good. We can be on our way once we're done eating. I need to run some errands, I'll drop you off on the way." Anya smiled at her son, delighted to know that he hadn't forgotten about Charlie. Charlie was the Wilsons' pet German Shepard. Before Fenton had left for London, the two were quite close.

ROY

At around 2 AM, Roy Hammond, Jorah Wilson's lawyer, was snapped out of his dreams by his Cell Phone's ringtone. He sat up on his bed and answered the call.

"Hello there, who's speaking please?"

The voice explained "Hi, Roy. I'm truly sorry to disturb you at this hour, but I need your help. Yesterday, sometime after my son came home, I received yet another one of those threatening emails-" Jorah was cut off by Roy, who was annoyed.

"Jorah, I've already told you. For the time being, the only thing we will do is ignore those emails. Joseph's not done anything apart from those emails either-" This time Roy was cut off.

"No, no. You're not getting the point. I have a feeling that Joseph is planning to harm my son. The timing bothers me. Joseph sent me that email only a couple of hours after Fenton reached home. I feel that he is somehow following my son's movements and is planning for a kidnap. Don't you agree?" prompted Jorah anxiously.

"Ok, I understand your concerns, Jorah. Let us talk about this in the morning. For now, your son is safe and sound in your residence, and no one can harm or take him. Until then, you try and get some sleep. Good night." said the lawyer.

"Well, I guess I agree. Good night." yawned the paranoid father.

Roy was a very understanding person. This time he was no different, and he agreed with Jorah. The fact that Joseph sent that email only a couple of hours after Fenton arrived home was no coincidence. Roy lay back down on his bed, thinking about the theory until he eventually fell back asleep.

He woke up the next morning with his mind still buzzing with ideas. How could Joseph have known when Fenton would come home? Where was he now? What was he going to do next? There were thousands of variables to consider. Too many for Roy to comprehend at once. He walked up to a cupboard and pulled out a dusty old briefcase. He opened it. Inside were two things: a gun and a picture of a young man, from his first ever case. He remembered it like it was yesterday. Coming home to meet up with his best friend, who was like a brother to him. Driving down the street in his shiny new sports car, having the time of their lives. And then the bang that came from a neighbouring window. A scream. A thud. And his best friend lying in his lap in front of him, blood oozing from his head. Dead.

The murderer had driven off cackling in his pickup truck, but not before Roy had snapped a clear picture of his face and vehicle. He went to the police and filed a case of first degree murder. The man was arrested and taken into custody and trial began shortly after. Roy served as the attorney for the prosecutor, that being his friend's family, and the defendant's lawyer was a man who Roy would never forget: Joseph May.

Both lawyers fought hard for their clients, but ultimately Roy won the case and the man was convicted. He was sentenced to death but somehow escaped his fate through some technicality. Roy had always suspected this technicality to be money. Since then he and Joseph had been bitter rivals in and out of the court. Joseph became known as a lawyer whose clients were notorious criminals and villains whereas Roy became known as a man of honor and duty. But to this day Roy never forgot his first case. And now he saw his chance to avenge his best friend and settle this once and for all. To protect his client's family and his client as well. To serve justice to all those who had been wronged by the clients of his greatest enemy. He picked up the gun, loaded it, and walked out of the house.

JORAH

As he walked, he brooded over the past 5 years of his life. Those were by far the most exhilarating days of his life, even more so than when he found out about his brother's lies on his own. Ten years after his brother's demise, he walked into the local police station and confessed to the crime out of pure guilt for committing it in the first place. He requested a full trial at the local court that would take place the following day. This news seemed to excite someone, as the lawyer who was fighting for the case against him, Joseph, documented each and every detail of the incident to the point that one could believe that it was his fake account that was true rather than what Jorah was saying. Yet some people still believed Joseph despite him not even physically being there. But the court still ruled in Jorah's favor anyway. Despite that, he was sentenced to six months in an asylum where he would receive therapy before being released. In those six months, a lot had changed. For one, his son had been moved to a boarding school far away in London and was soon approaching high school. His wealth that would have been his in normal circumstances ended up going to some distant cousin of his whom he barely knew, and his family had moved to a modest four-bedroom semi-detached house. But he didn't mind it. The only concern in his head was to strengthen his relationship with his son.

Jorah had formed a mediocre relationship with Fenton, at best. He had spent most of the past fourteen years in legal trouble over the inheritance or being threatened into investing in lucrative stocks, which was the reason he lost his inheritance to some seventh cousin or someone. He was thoroughly annoyed by that. Shortly afterward, his trial happened, and he moved on with life.

As Jorah continued his walk, he couldn't help but reflect on the twists and turns his life had taken. The memories of his brother's betrayal and the subsequent confession weighed heavily on his mind. He had always looked up to his brother, believing him to be a paragon of virtue. Discovering the truth had shattered his world, and the guilt of his own actions had gnawed at him for years. The decision to confess had been a difficult one, but he had hoped it would bring him some semblance of peace.

The trial had been a whirlwind of emotions. Joseph, the lawyer, had been relentless in his pursuit of justice.

His meticulous documentation of the incident had painted a vivid picture of the crime, making it hard for anyone to doubt his version of events. Jorah had felt like a spectator in his own trial, watching as his fate was decided by others. Despite the court ruling in his favor, the sentence of six months in an asylum had been a bitter pill to swallow for both Jorah and his lawyer, Roy. The therapy sessions had been grueling, forcing him to confront his demons and come to terms with his actions.

During his time in the asylum, Jorah had missed out on many important moments in his son's life. Fenton had grown up so quickly, and Jorah felt a pang of regret for not being there for him. The move to Manchester had been a fresh start for the family, but it had also meant leaving behind the life they had known. The four-bedroom house was a far cry from the grand estate they had once called home, but it was a place where they could rebuild their lives.

Jorah's relationship with Fenton had always been strained. The legal battles and financial troubles had taken a toll on their bond. Jorah had tried to be a good father, but the constant stress and pressure had made it difficult. He had often found himself preoccupied with his own problems, leaving little time for his son.
Fenton, in turn, had grown distant, seeking solace in his own pursuits.

As they walked together, Jorah tried to bridge the gap between them. He asked Fenton about school, his friends, and his interests. Fenton responded politely, but there was a noticeable lack of enthusiasm in his voice. Jorah couldn't help but feel a sense of failure as a father. He had hoped that their time in Manchester would bring them closer, but it seemed that the wounds of the past were not so easily healed.

Charlie, their loyal dog, provided a welcome distraction. The playful bark and wagging tail brought a smile to Jorah's face. He watched as Fenton threw a stick for Charlie to fetch, the simple act of play bringing a moment of joy to their otherwise somber walk. Jorah realised that he needed to make more of an effort to connect with his son. The past could not be changed, but the future was still within his control.

Determined to mend their relationship, Jorah decided to take a more active role in Fenton's life. He started attending school events, cheering from the sidelines at football matches, and helping with homework. Slowly but surely, the walls between them began to crumble. Fenton started to open up, sharing his dreams and aspirations with his father. Jorah listened intently, offering support and encouragement.

The bond between them grew stronger with each passing day. Jorah found solace in the simple moments they shared, whether it was a walk in the park or a quiet evening at home. He realized that being a father was not about grand gestures or material wealth, but about being present and showing love. The mistakes of the past could not be undone, but they could learn from them and build a better future together.

As the day drew to a close, Jorah felt a sense of accomplishment. He had taken the first steps towards rebuilding his relationship with Fenton. They had shared a meaningful conversation, and Jorah had seen a glimpse of the bond they could have. He knew it would take time and effort, but he was committed to making it work.

"Fenton, I think it's time for me to head home," Jorah said, breaking the comfortable silence that had settled between them.

Fenton looked up, a hint of surprise in his eyes. "Already? I thought we could walk a bit longer."

Jorah smiled weakly as he looked into his son's eyes. "You can continue the walk with Charlie if you want to. It's good for both of you. I'll see you at home."

Fenton nodded, a small smile playing on his lips. "Alright, Dad. I'll see you later."

Jorah watched as Fenton continued down the path, Charlie trotting happily beside him. He felt a sense of peace as he turned and made his way back home. The day had been a step in the right direction, and he was hopeful for the future. As he walked, he reflected on the journey they had been on and the progress they had made. It wasn't perfect, but it was a start.

When Jorah reached home, he felt a sense of contentment. He knew that there were still challenges ahead, but he was ready to face them. With Fenton by his side, he felt a renewed sense of purpose and a deep, abiding love that would guide them through whatever came next. The past was behind them, and the future was theirs to create.

JOSEPH

Early in the gloomy Manchester morning, the committed lawyer of Sylas Wilson—before he died—pulled up before the Wilson estate in his car. He sat in a sleek black saloon, drumming his fingers on the wheel as he waited for the boy to exit the house.

Joseph May was waiting for Fenton Wilson, but not with good intentions. Joseph wanted to teach Jorah a lesson. He smirked to himself, thinking, "You take my client, I take your son." Joseph checked his watch eagerly.

"Where is he? I thought he would go out first thing in the morning to see his friends. It's nine AM already!" the lawyer muttered to himself. Finally, after about half an hour, the door of the Wilson estate opened, and out stepped Fenton—followed by Anya.

"Oh, come on! Why did you have to bring your mother into this? All because of her, all my waiting was for nothing!" yelled the frustrated lawyer after punching the steering wheel. Joseph shoved the idling Mercedes-Benz E-Class into drive and sped off into the Manchester streets.

Joseph May had always been a man who thrived on control. As Sylas Wilson's legal representative, he'd been privy to the man's deepest secrets and darkest dealings. When Sylas died unexpectedly, leaving Jorah—his younger, less ruthless associate—to pick up the pieces, Joseph had been furious. He believed Jorah's incompetence had cost him his most lucrative client.

For months, Joseph stewed in his anger, nursing his grudge like a fine wine. He'd heard rumors about the Wilson family from his contacts—how Anya had distanced herself from Sylas's shady dealings, how Fenton was oblivious to his father's dark legacy. It was perfect. They were vulnerable, unsuspecting. Joseph saw them as the ideal targets to channel his frustration.

But this morning had not gone according to plan. He'd spent hours parked outside the estate, waiting for the boy to leave alone. Instead, Anya had ruined everything by accompanying her son. Joseph's plans required precision, and Anya's presence complicated matters. Frustrated, he drove aimlessly through the city, his mind racing with thoughts of revenge.

Back at the Wilson estate, Anya had no idea she'd just thwarted a potential threat. She was focused on getting Fenton ready for the day.

"Did you pack everything for your project?" she asked, brushing a stray lock of hair out of her face.
Fenton nodded, slinging his backpack over his shoulder. "Yeah, I'm all set. Can I go now?"
"Not so fast," Anya said with a smile. "I'll drop you off on my way to the store."
"Mom, I'm not a kid," Fenton groaned. "I can walk."
"Humor me," she said, her tone leaving no room for argument.

As they left the house together, Joseph's black Mercedes was nowhere in sight. Anya glanced around the street, a faint unease prickling at the back of her mind. She dismissed it quickly. After all, Manchester was always bustling with cars; why should she feel anything was out of place?

Joseph, meanwhile, had pulled over at a quiet café. He ordered a coffee and sat by the window, staring blankly at the busy street outside. His mind was a storm of frustration and determination. He couldn't afford another failure. If he wanted to send Jorah a message, he'd have to be smarter—more calculating.

He pulled out his phone and scrolled through his contacts until he found a name: Gareth. Gareth was an old acquaintance, a man with a reputation for getting things done discreetly. Joseph hesitated for a moment before pressing the call button.

"Joseph," Gareth's gravelly voice answered after a few rings. "It's been a while. What do you need?"
"A favor," Joseph said, his voice steady despite the turmoil inside him. "I need you to... keep an eye on someone for me. A boy and his mother."

There was a pause on the other end. "Sounds like you're stirring trouble," Gareth said. "But I'm listening."
Joseph outlined his plan in vague terms, careful not to reveal too much. By the time he hung up, he felt a renewed sense of control. Gareth would do the groundwork, and Joseph would remain in the shadows, pulling the strings.

Over the next few days, Gareth kept a close watch on the Wilson family. He observed their routines, noting when they left the house, where they went, and who they interacted with. He reported back to Joseph every evening, his updates painting a detailed picture of their lives.

"The kid's got a pretty standard schedule," Gareth said during one such call. "School, friends, home. The mom's a bit more unpredictable, but she's cautious. Always checking her surroundings."

Joseph listened intently, his mind working overtime to craft the next phase of his plan. He wanted to strike at the perfect moment—a moment that would leave Jorah reeling.

One morning, as Anya was leaving the house to run errands, she spotted a figure lingering near the edge of their property. Her instincts kicked in, and she slowed her steps, pretending not to notice. The man didn't move, his gaze fixed on the street ahead.

Anya's heart raced as she got into her car. She locked the doors and pulled out her phone, snapping a quick photo of the stranger. She couldn't shake the feeling that something was wrong. As she drove away, she made a mental note to show the picture to Jorah later.

When she returned home that afternoon, the man was gone, but the sense of unease lingered. Anya decided it was time to have a serious conversation with Jorah. She couldn't ignore the signs any longer.
"Do you think it could be someone from Sylas's past?" Anya asked that evening, showing Jorah the photo she'd taken.

Jorah studied the image, his brow furrowed. "It's possible. Sylas had a lot of enemies, and not all of them went away when he did."
"We need to be careful," Anya said. "I don't want Fenton caught up in any of this."
Jorah nodded, placing a reassuring hand on her shoulder. "We'll keep an eye out. But for now, let's not jump to conclusions. It might be nothing."
Anya wanted to believe him, but the gnawing fear in her chest wouldn't let her rest. She knew deep down that this was just the beginning of something far more dangerous.

FENTON

After briefing a very groggy Jorah on where they were headed, Fenton and his mother, Anya, stepped out of the door. It was a crisp and cool morning, with a spot of rain. The air was filled with the faint scent of dew on the pavements. The familiar streets of Manchester were quiet, almost eerily so.

Fenton noticed a sleek black saloon whizzing past, its tires screeching as it took a sharp turn at the end of the street. "Woah, he must be in a hurry," Fenton commented, watching the car disappear around the corner. He had no idea that his fate could have taken a very different turn—had it not been for his mother, he might have found himself inside that very car.

The two of them walked briskly towards the Wilsons' car, parked neatly along the curb. The car gleamed under the pale sunlight, a stark contrast to the darker, gloomier atmosphere of the city. Anya unlocked the car with a beep, and the pair climbed in.

As Fenton settled into his seat and clicked on his seatbelt, he glanced out of the window. The slow, methodical way the streets of Manchester moved stood in such stark contrast to the chaos he had become accustomed to in London. It was the first time in nearly a year that he had found himself back in his hometown, and it felt like the world was moving at half the speed he had gotten used to.

"I can't believe how... quiet it is," he said softly, more to himself than to his mother. He watched the pedestrians strolling down the pavement at a leisurely pace, chatting to one another, sipping their coffee from takeaway cups. It was all so different from the hustle and bustle of London, where everyone seemed to be in a rush, pushing past one another to get to wherever they were going.

Anya glanced at him in the rearview mirror, with a small smile. "It's always been like this. You've just been away for too long," she said, a hint of sadness creeping into her voice.

Fenton leaned back, his thoughts drifting. Maybe if he had had a sibling, life would have turned out differently. He could have stayed in Manchester with his parents, "No way would they send both of their children to a boarding school", Fenton thought. He really wanted to go back to growing up in the same house, on the same quiet streets he had known his whole life. The thought felt strange, like an alternative reality, something that could have happened but never did. He shook the thought off and sighed softly, glancing at his mother.

"You miss it here, don't you?" Anya asked, her eyes flickering to him in the rearview mirror. She was a woman of few words when it came to emotions, but there were moments when she allowed the tenderness to show through, especially with her son.

He shrugged, not really sure how to put it into words. Did he miss Manchester? It felt like a lifetime ago since he had left. "I don't know," he replied after a moment. "I guess I miss how simple things were. I didn't appreciate it at the time, but... London's different. Everyone's always moving. Here, it feels like people actually take time to breathe."

Anya chuckled softly. "That's Manchester for you. People have always been different here."

They drove in silence for a while, the city slowly passing them by. Fenton kept looking out the window, his mind replaying different memories at every turn. He remembered the park he used to play in as a kid, the quiet afternoons spent riding his bike down the streets, the evenings when his father would come home from work and the three of them would sit down to dinner together. Life had been slower, more predictable. There was a part of him that longed for that predictability, especially after the whirlwind of change he had gone through in London.

"Do you think I'll ever come back?" Fenton asked suddenly, his voice breaking the silence.

Anya didn't answer immediately. She kept her eyes on the road, her hands gripping the steering wheel a little tighter. "I don't know, Fenton. Maybe. Maybe one day. But not now."

Fenton nodded, even though he didn't fully understand why. After all, he didn't really know what was keeping him in London. But he knew better than to push his mother for an explanation. She was the type who carried her burdens quietly, never letting anyone see how much weight she bore on her shoulders.

Before he knew it, they reached the edge of the city. The streets became wider and the buildings gave way to patches of green. It was a different side of Manchester, one that

Fenton had almost forgotten existed. He realized, with a pang of nostalgia, that this was where he had spent most of his childhood, playing football with his friends in the park, riding his bike down the quiet streets.

As they drove through, he couldn't help but feel a sense of loss. London had been exciting, yes, but it had also been isolating. In Manchester, everything had felt more connected, more real. There had been a sense of community, of belonging, that he hadn't found in the big city.

"Do you ever regret it?" Fenton asked, surprising himself with the question.

Anya raised an eyebrow. "Regret what?"

"Moving me to London," Fenton clarified. "Making me leave all this behind."

Anya was quiet for a moment, her fingers tapping lightly on the steering wheel as she considered her response. "Sometimes," she admitted. "But... life changes. You couldn't stay here forever, Fenton. You know that."

"I guess," he said, though he wasn't sure he really believed it. It felt like he had left something important behind, something he couldn't get back.

They drove on in silence again, and Fenton let his mind drift. He thought about his old friends, the ones he hadn't spoken to in years. He wondered what they were doing now, if they had stayed in Manchester or if they, too, had moved on to bigger cities, chasing new opportunities. He wondered if they remembered him, or if he had become just another name from their past, a fleeting memory that had faded with time.

The Hyundai Tucson hummed softly as it made its way down the road, the steady rhythm of raindrops on the window lulling Fenton into a trance-like state. The world outside the window seemed to blur, and for a moment, he felt like he had been transported somewhere else entirely, somewhere caught between the past and the present.

"I used to think about what it would be like if I had a brother or sister," Fenton said suddenly, breaking the silence. "Like... maybe they could have stayed here with you and Dad while I went to London. Things would have been different, you know?"

Anya glanced at him, her expression softening. "Maybe. But you don't need to think about what could have been. Life is what it is, and we can't change the past. You're here now, and that's all that matters."

Fenton smiled faintly, though he wasn't entirely convinced. He couldn't help but think about all the different paths his life could have taken, all the choices he had made that had led him to this moment.

Before he knew it, the car had stopped in a parking space. He looked up and found that they had arrived at the local Tesco.

"Come on, let's finish this shopping list," his mother called,

"Hello, Earth to Fenton?"

Fenton shook the thoughts out of his head, "Coming, mum!" He called as he shut the car door behind him.

81

CHAPTER XIII

ANYA

Anya Wilson pulled her phone out of her purse and quickly sent a message to her husband. It read, "I think I saw Joseph's car drive past our house. It was a black Mercedes saloon." Once she saw that her son had reached her side, she took a trolley and pulled up the shopping list on her phone.

"Come on, Fenton. The faster we finish, the faster you meet your friends."
For the whole duration of the trip, Anya was mostly quiet. Her mind kept churning the sight of the black car over and over in her head. Her quietness was so unusual that even Fenton had asked her a couple of times about the matter.
"Mom, are you sure you're okay?" he asked, pushing the trolley beside her.
"Yes, I'm fine," she replied, giving him a small smile that didn't quite reach her eyes. "I'm just thinking about a work issue."

Fenton didn't seem convinced, but he didn't push further. They moved through the aisles, tossing in boxes of cereal, fresh vegetables, and the occasional snack. Anya's eyes flicked around the store, scanning the faces of shoppers and glancing at the entrance every few seconds. Her unease was palpable.

As they reached the frozen food section, her phone buzzed. She glanced at the screen and saw a message from her husband, Jorah: "Are you sure? Joseph hasn't been around for years. Maybe it's someone else?"

Anya's lips tightened as she typed back: "I know it sounds crazy, but I'm certain. The license plate was almost identical to his old one. What if he's back?"

She hit send and slipped the phone back into her purse, her hands trembling slightly. Memories of Joseph flooded her mind—memories she had worked so hard to bury. The way he used to stare at her, his voice smooth and cold, and the threats he'd made when she finally cut him out of their lives. She had hoped those days were behind them.

"Mom, can I grab some ice cream?" Fenton's voice snapped her out of her thoughts.

"Sure, go ahead," she said, watching him jog to the freezer. Her phone buzzed again. Another message from Jorah: "Let's not jump to conclusions. Finish shopping and come home. We'll talk then."

She nodded to herself. Maybe he was right. Maybe she was overreacting. But as they checked out and headed to the car, the nagging feeling in her gut wouldn't go away.

The drive home was uneventful, but Anya couldn't shake the sense of being watched. Every black car they passed made her stomach twist, though none of them turned out to be the Mercedes she'd seen earlier.

When they pulled into the driveway, she glanced around the street, her eyes scanning for anything out of place. Nothing.

"Go on inside, Fenton. I'll bring the bags," she said, her

voice firmer than usual.

"Okay," he said, bounding up the steps.

Anya opened the trunk and began unloading. She had just grabbed the last bag when she heard the faint hum of an engine. Her head whipped around, and there it was—the black Mercedes, parked halfway down the street. The driver's window was tinted, hiding whoever was inside.

She froze, the grocery bag dangling from her fingers. A long moment passed before the car pulled away slowly, disappearing around the corner. Her pulse pounded in her ears as she hurried inside and locked the door behind her.

"You're imagining things," Jorah said later that evening. They were sitting in the living room, the TV playing in the background while Fenton worked on a school project upstairs.

"I'm not," Anya insisted. "It's the same car. And now it's been on our street twice."

"Even if it is Joseph's old car, it doesn't mean he's driving it. Cars change hands all the time. It could be a coincidence."

Anya rubbed her temples, frustration bubbling inside her. "You didn't see the way he used to look at me, Jorah. He's not the type to let go easily. What if he's come back for revenge?"

Jorah sighed and reached for her hand. "If it'll make you feel better, I'll call the police and report the car. But we can't jump to conclusions. Let's not let this ruin our peace."

She nodded reluctantly, though her mind was far from at ease.

That night, Anya lay awake, staring at the ceiling. Every creak of the house, every rustle of the wind outside, set her on edge. She checked the locks three times before finally climbing into bed, but sleep refused to come.

Around 2 a.m., she heard it: the faint growl of an engine outside. Her heart raced as she slipped out of bed and crept to the window. Peeking through the curtain, she saw it again—the black Mercedes, idling at the curb.

For a moment, she considered waking Jorah, but something stopped her. Instead, she grabbed her phone and snapped a photo of the car. As she zoomed in, she thought she saw movement inside, but the tinted windows made it impossible to tell for sure.

Suddenly, the car's headlights flicked on, and it sped off into the night. Anya's hands trembled as she lowered the phone. She knew now that this was no coincidence.
The next morning, she showed the photo to Jorah. "This isn't just me being paranoid. Whoever's driving that car is watching us."

Jorah studied the picture, his jaw tightening. "Okay. I'll call the police. But you need to stay calm, Anya. We don't want to scare Fenton."

She nodded, though calm was the last thing she felt.
Over the next few days, Anya tried to go about her routine, but the black car was always in the back of her mind. She kept her phone close, ready to call for help if needed. Jorah had reported the car to the police, but without more

information, there wasn't much they could do.

One afternoon, while Fenton was at a friend's house, Anya decided to run a quick errand. As she pulled out of the driveway, she noticed the Mercedes parked at the end of the street again. Her hands gripped the steering wheel tightly as she drove past it, glancing in her rearview mirror. Sure enough, the car pulled out and began following her.

Her pulse quickened. She took a few turns, trying to convince herself it was just a coincidence, but the Mercedes stayed behind her. Panic set in as she realized she needed to do something.
Spotting a gas station up ahead, she made a sudden decision and pulled in, parking near the entrance. She grabbed her phone and dialed Jorah.

"The car's following me," she said, her voice shaking. "I'm at the gas station on Cedar Avenue. Can you come?"
"I'm on my way," Jorah said. "Stay in the car and lock the doors."
Anya hung up and looked around. The Mercedes had stopped across the street, its engine still running. She couldn't see the driver, but she could feel their eyes on her. Her breathing grew shallow as she debated what to do.

Minutes felt like hours as she waited for Jorah. Finally, she saw his car pull into the lot. Relief washed over her as he parked beside her and got out. She stepped out of her car and ran to him.

"It's there," she said, pointing to the Mercedes. But when they turned to look, the car was gone.

Jorah sighed, wrapping an arm around her shoulders. "Let's go home. We'll figure this out together."
That night, Anya received an anonymous text message. It read: "You can't hide forever."

Her blood ran cold. She stared at the screen, her mind racing. Who was this? Joseph? Or someone else entirely? And what did they want?

Just then, the power went out, plunging the house into darkness. Anya's heart pounded as she heard a faint knock at the front door. She turned to Jorah, who was already reaching for the baseball bat he kept by the couch.

"Stay here," he whispered.

But Anya couldn't shake the feeling that whoever was out there wasn't going to wait for an invitation.
The knock came again, louder this time. And then, through the silence, they heard the unmistakable sound of a window shattering upstairs.

CHAPTER XIV

JORAH

He walked up the stairs silently, clutching his baseball bat. It was quite a ridiculous weapon, but it would have to do. He started searching the rooms upstairs, when he heard a sudden sharp breath come from Fenton's room. Gotcha. He stormed into the room, meeting the invader head on.

"What are you doing here?" he asked.

"I-I'm here to i-inform you about the case, yes, the case against you, for, uh..."

"For my brother's death" replied Jorah.
"Yes, yes. That's right. Your brother's death. His murder rather."
"Who sent you?"
"Joseph. Joseph May." the intruder said.

"Sylas' lawyer. So he's been reduced to sending buffoons like you to threaten me. Let me guess, you entered my son's room, hoping to catch him off guard and take him hostage. Then you would demand a ransom to get him back, in return for which you wouldn't file the case, right?"

"Yes, sir. Th-that was the plan, I think." he said nervously.
"I don't think so. You, or your, hmm, boss, rather, failed to win the case against me and is now attempting to take my son hostage to murder him in order to avenge a criminal."

"N-No sir, Joseph would never do that."
"Oh really? Should I call the police then?"

In a sudden flash the intruder drew a dagger and attacked Jorah, who managed to parry him with the baseball bat in the nick of time.

"You gonna get me with that?" asked the intruder.
"No. I'll get you with this." replied Jorah.

Saying that he dropped his bat and pulled a dagger from his pocket, tossing the sheath on the ground and going straight for the intruder's head. Sparks flew as the daggers clashed against each other, shining in the light. As the opponents cut each other, blood spilled around the room. Jorah heard the door open, and caught a brief glimpse of his wife and son watching in shock as he fought the intruder, ultimately pinning him down on the wall before springing into action again as the man reached out to grab his throat. He yanked the intruder forward before ripping his mask off of his face and revealing a square cut jawline and a small narrow nose between his beady eyes.

"S-Sir. P-Please d-d-don't k-kill me" he stammered.

"I'll spare you this once. Consider it payment for letting me win the case. Now get out of my house." said Jorah.

The man bolted down the steps and out the main door.

"Dad?" asked Fenton shyly.
"Yes?"
"Who was that?"

"Someone who wanted to harm you. Don't worry, you're safe now."

"Fenton, stay here. Me and your dad need to talk. Privately." said Anya.

They walked downstairs, the steps trailing droplets of blood from the man's wounds.

"What was that about?" asked Anya in an accusatory but fearful tone.

"What d'you mean?"

"Why were you fighting him? With a dagger of all things?"

"You think I'd let him loose, without putting up a fight? Trust me, I've learned my lesson after Sylas. I will not let him loose if he intends to harm my son or anyone close to me."

"Sylas was close to you. But you murdered him."

"Sylas was different. He was a criminal. A liar. A fraud and a crook. He got what he deserved."

"You said you called that mercy. Does that mean you thought he deserved worse?"

"Let's not talk about Sylas now. He's dead and gone. Lost in the past."

"Okay"

Jorah sat in his room, trying to contemplate his next move. His first instinct, call Roy.

"Good evening. Sorry to call you so late."

"What's the problem?" asked Roy calmly.

"Joseph's sending mercenaries to my house to kidnap and harm my son. Can you do something about it?"

"I could file a restraining order, but I doubt it'll hardly affect him. Can you tell me how the mercenary looked?"

"Square cut jaw, beady eyes, big forehead., black hair. He

looked to be around thirty.”

“I’ll see what I can do. Let me contact Joseph to see if he has anything to do with it first. Mercenaries aren’t exactly known for being honest.”

“Fair point. Good night.”

“I’ll call you when I’m done. Good night.”

A few hours later, Jorah’s phone rang again. It was Roy.

“So? What did he say?”

“Nothing. I’ve been calling him, emailing him, and sending him messages. No response.”

“Something’s up.”

“I know. Joseph isn’t normally like this. He’s usually prompt and ready with an answer to everything.”

“Send me screenshots of your calling lists, emails, and private messages to Joseph.”

“What? Why?”

“Just do it.”

Saying that, he cut the phone.

“Seriously, Jorah?”

He turned around and saw that his wife had woken up.

“What?”

“Don’t you trust your own lawyer?”

“No. I don’t trust anybody’s words without direct proof. I want to know if he’s hiding something from me.”

‘Well, there’s a limit.”

“That limit is you and Fenton.”

“Okay. But you have to learn to trust people. Everyone isn’t like your brother. There are honest people out there.”

“My brother taught me one thing in his entire life. Trust no one."

Epilogue

He walked on the rainy streets, breathing heavily from running so fast. That Jorah guy was pretty scary for your average dad. He looked over at his wrist, which was dripping blood.It was paining slightly. The cut itself wasn't that deep because it was made in the heat of the moment. He felt lucky the man didn't know what he was doing for the most part. But now he knew what his boss was up to, and his identity. He ran the risk of getting arrested for breaking and entering. At least his name was still unknown. He walked over to a sleek black sedan that was parked in an alleyway and got in.

His face was dripping with water and sweat as he got into the car. What was his boss gonna say when he realised that the mission failed? Would he even get paid a quarter of the agreed amount? Joseph was quite well known for being ruthless towards the employees he'd hired, particularly the mercenaries, as he always expected top notch performance from those he hired. That would come as no surprise as he always hired mercenaries with a reputation for their work, especially in jobs such as these. But he had known Joseph for well over ten years now. And the man was quite the penny pincher. At first glance, Joseph looked like an ordinary lawyer from the middle class who worked on cases that weren't that significant. But those in his inner circle knew that he had quite the reputation in the criminal underworld of Manchester for being one of the best criminal lawyers out there. So it came as no surprise when he was hired by Sylas Wilson, a notorious criminal overlord who managed to avoid capture with his immense web of lies while simultaneously sitting atop a mountain of money.

Joseph was obviously paid copious amounts of money for helping Sylas get around the law and manage his business. But unlike his employer, Joseph decided to keep his fortune safe, engaging in illicit activities of his own. He converted most of the money into gold bars to store in his own house rather than putting into a bank to remove the risk of getting on the government's radar. And he soon followed in his employer's footsteps, employing his own mercenaries and guards to keep him safe and do missions. And Gareth was the first one he contacted for that. Gareth's original job was to hire and manage the mercenary side of Sylas' business, but after Sylas' death, the entire business was dissolved and Gareth was eventually left unemployed. He found a gig at a small convenience store as a security guard where he worked briefly before being called back by Joseph for this mission.

As he was reminiscing about his time under Sylas, his prime time, as he liked to call it, he came upon the modest suburban home where Joseph had taken residence. He walked in.

"Joseph? I'm back. And... the mission failed."
No response.
"Joseph? Where are you?"

Still nothing. Just the wind howling outside. He decided to take a look in his office. He walked in and opened the door which was left unlocked. An unusual thing for Joseph to do. He walked forward towards his boss' desk

"Joseph? You alright there boss?"
And then he stood still in shock.
"What... no. No no no no no. This can't be."

There in front of him, on the desk, with a hole through his head, was Joseph, surrounded by a pool of blood with a note:

"For Jorah".

Gareth grunted in dismay. Seriously? How much more would he have to deal with?

He walked out into the garage to take his truck for a swing but instead found another body lying against it. It was a man, holding a gun in his hand. Yeah, that's the killer all right. He moved closer for a better look. The man had an ID in his pocket from the law firm where he worked. It said he was a private lawyer currently in the employment of an anonymous person. His name was written in block letters on the top. Roy Hammond.

THE END